Harriet Castor
Ballet Magic on Stage

Illustrated by Chris Fisher

PUFFIN BOOKS

PUFFIN BOOKS

Published by the Penguin Group
Penguin Books Ltd, 27 Wrights Lane, London W8 5TZ, England
Penguin Putnam Inc., 375 Hudson Street, New York, New York 10014, USA
Penguin Books Australia Ltd, Ringwood, Victoria, Australia
Penguin Books Canada Ltd, 10 Alcorn Avenue, Toronto, Ontario, Canada M4V 3B2
Penguin Books (NZ) Ltd, Private Bag 102902, NSMC, Auckland, New Zealand

On the World Wide Web at: www.penguin.com

Penguin Books Ltd, Registered Offices: Harmondsworth, Middlesex, England

First published 1999
1 3 5 7 9 10 8 6 4 2

Printed in Hong Kong by Midas Printing Ltd

British Library Cataloguing in Publication Data
A CIP catalogue record for this book is available from the British Library

ISBN 0-140-38480-4

For Laura and Erica,
who love ballet too

On Fridays, Jess went to ballet with her best friend, Flo. This week, when they walked into the changing room, they found everyone crowding round a poster on the wall. It showed two ballet dancers in wonderful costumes, and it said that the National Ballet

Company was coming to the Grand Theatre in two weeks' time.

"*My* mother's already booked tickets," said Primrose Pettifer.

Jess rolled her eyes. Primrose loved showing off.

"And," added Primrose, admiring herself in the mirror, "we're not going to be in normal seats. We'll have a box all to ourselves."

Just then a white-haired lady put her head round the changing-room door and smiled a sparkly smile. It was Miss Angelica Twirl, the ballet teacher. Her sister, Miss Ethel Twirl, played the piano in class.

"Come along, dears!" said Miss Angelica.

Miss Angelica and Miss Ethel,

Jess and Flo had discovered, were rather special. No one else in the class knew it, but they could do magic. It made ballet lessons extra fun.

Now, when they went into the hall, Jess and Flo found two strangers there with the Miss Twirls – a glamorous-looking lady and a grumpy-looking man. Jess thought they seemed oddly familiar.

Flo nudged her. "It's the people from the poster!"

Jess stared. Flo was right.

"Children," said Miss Angelica, taking the glamorous lady's hand, "I would like you to meet Margot Fountain. Margot is a ballet dancer."

"A real live ballerina," Flo whispered to Jess, her eyes wide.

"She dances with the National Ballet. If you've seen the poster you'll know they will be performing soon at the Grand Theatre," said Miss Ethel. "And because we used to be Margot's ballet teachers, she

has kindly agreed to come and dance for you today."

Miss Angelica told everyone to sit cross-legged on the floor while Margot Fountain put on her ballet shoes. The grumpy-looking man was her partner from the National Ballet. His name was Julian Joompalot.

When Miss Ethel was ready at the piano, Margot and Julian began to dance. They leapt and spun and did all sorts of tricky steps. Margot danced on her toes. Julian lifted her high in the air. It was the best dancing Jess had ever seen. Julian still looked grumpy though.

"Is he always that cross, do you think?" Jess whispered to Flo.

When Margot and Julian had finished, everyone clapped. Then Miss Angelica said, "A week on Tuesday, Margot is giving her first performance as the princess in *The Sleeping Beauty*. Miss Ethel and I will be arranging a trip to see it. Would anyone like to come?"

"Me!" cried Flo straight away,

waving her hand in the air. Jess shot her hand up too. So did everyone else in the class. Except, that is, for Primrose Pettifer.

"I shan't need to come with you," declared Primrose loudly. "That's the night Mummy's taking me. We'll be sitting in a box, you know," she added, looking at the

Miss Twirls to see if they were impressed.

But Miss Angelica and Miss Ethel were too busy making lists and giving instructions to take any notice of Primrose. There was a lot of organizing to do. Everyone would have to ask their parents if they could go. After that, Miss Angelica would have to ring the theatre and book the tickets.

The next Friday, before the lesson began, Miss Ethel went round the class asking if everyone had a lift to the theatre.

"My mum and dad are busy that night," said Jess. She was worried this might mean she couldn't go.

"And my mum doesn't have a car," said Flo, looking anxious too.

"Don't worry, dears," said Miss Ethel, "I'm sure we can find someone else to take you both." She frowned and looked at her list. "Most of the cars are full. Except . . .

ah, yes –" her finger stopped at a
name – "Primrose Pettifer's. I
wonder if her mother and father
would mind . . ."

While Miss Ethel went to ask
Primrose, Jess made a face at Flo.

"I don't want to go with
Primrose," said Jess. "Do you?"

"Not much," admitted Flo. "But it'll be worth it if we get to see Margot Fountain again."

Just then they heard Primrose's voice. "Of course it's a jolly big car," she was saying, "but we can't possibly take anyone else. My party dress would get crumpled."

Miss Ethel came back looking cross. "Never mind," she said to Jess and Flo. "You'll just have to come with Miss Angelica and me. Our car is rather small, but I'm sure we'll be able to manage."

Jess grinned. "We'll breathe in," she said.

On Tuesday night, Jess and Flo arrived at the Miss Twirls' house in good time. Jess lifted the ballerina-shaped knocker and knocked on the front door.

"Jessica, Florence, come in, come in," said Miss Angelica, opening the door and beaming at them.

She was dressed in a long shiny
gown and her dangly earrings were
little gold ballet shoes.

Miss Ethel was dressed up too.
She had a large feather in her hair
and a glittery necklace. "It's time
we were off, dears," she said. "I like

to be in my seat nice and early so that I can read the programme."

"Now, where did I put the car keys?" said Miss Angelica, peering round.

Just then the phone rang. "Spells and spillikins, who can that be?"

muttered Miss Ethel, and went to answer it. A moment later she came back, looking flustered.

"That was Margot Fountain," she said. "She's very upset. Something's wrong – though she wouldn't tell me what. Angelica, she wants us to go and see her before the show starts."

"Then, Ethel, there's no time to lose," said Miss Angelica, who had found the keys and was putting on her long evening cloak. She turned to Jess and Flo. "And there won't be time to pop back for you two, so I'm afraid you'll have to come with us, dears. Hurry!"

The car was small, but Jess, Flo and the Miss Twirls somehow

squashed in, and Miss Angelica
drove to the theatre at top speed.
She parked round the back and
they went in at the stage door.

"Wow!" whispered Flo as the
stage door guard ushered them
through. "It's just as if we were
ballerinas too!"

Up in her dressing room, they found Margot Fountain in floods of tears. "It's my understudy," she sobbed. "Tanya Turnova. She's always been jealous of me. And just now, as I was coming out of the wardrobe mistress's room, I heard her say to someone that tonight isn't only my first night as princess

– it'll be my last too. Something bad's going to happen to me, so that tomorrow *she'll* be the princess instead!"

"What is it, this bad thing?" asked Miss Angelica, passing Margot a fresh handkerchief.

"That's the trouble," wailed Margot. "I don't know!"

"Well, don't fret," said Miss
Ethel. "We'll find out." She thought

hard. Then she said, "We must split up and search the theatre. We need to find Turnova – and keep an eye out for anything that looks odd or suspicious. I'll search downstairs. Angelica, you search this floor. Jessica and Florence, try upstairs."

Jess liked the idea of turning detective. It sounded exciting – but a bit scary too. "What if anyone asks why we're snooping around?" she said.

"Ah," said Miss Ethel. "I hadn't thought of that."

"Hurry!" sobbed Margot. "Please!"

"I've got an idea," said Miss Angelica. She rummaged in her handbag and produced a pair of opera glasses. She waved one hand over them, muttering something that Jess couldn't quite catch, then she put them to her eyes and stared at Jess. Jess felt a strange tingly feeling that started at the top of her head and spread all the way down to her feet. Flo gasped and clapped a hand over her mouth.

"What?" said Jess.

Flo pointed to the mirror. "Have
a look."

Jess looked. At first, what she saw
didn't make any sense. There was
her top, all blue and white stripes.
And there were her best trousers,
matching blue. The only thing
was, there was no *her* inside them.

Her cuffs had no hands at the ends. And above the collar, where the face should have been, there was an empty space.

"Bother!" said Miss Angelica. "I've forgotten how to make the clothes invisible too."

Jess turned round. Miss Angelica had already made Miss Ethel and Flo disappear. Now Miss Ethel's sleeve lifted and the opera glasses floated through the air. Jess supposed she must be holding them up to her eyes, so she could put the spell on Miss Angelica.

"Never mind," came Miss Ethel's voice, as Miss Angelica's face began to fade. "There's only twenty minutes until the show starts. This

26

will have to do. Let's get searching.
We'll meet back in this room in ten
minutes. Take care girls!"

Jess and Flo, still feeling a little
tingly, and giggling every time they

looked at one another – or, rather, at where one another *should* have been – set off up the stairs and through the shadowy corridors of the theatre.

Coming round one corner, Jess stopped suddenly. "Look!" she whispered. She pointed; though all she could see was her sleeve waggling in front of her. "It's Tanya Turnova's dressing room!"

The door was ajar. "Let's listen at the crack," hissed Flo.

They crept forward and listened.

"Do you hear anything?" came Flo's voice again.

Jess shook her head, and then remembered that Flo couldn't see her. "No," she whispered. "I think

it's empty. Perhaps we should go in
and look round."

Nervously, Jess pushed the door
open.

The room was like Margot's, but
messier. It was strewn with costumes

and headdresses and ballet shoes. On the table was a big box of make-up and some "Good Luck" cards.

"Look for something odd or suspicious," said Jess.

"I'm not sure what that could be," said Flo.

"Nor am I," said Jess, "but I reckon we'll know if we find it."

At that moment they heard footsteps coming along the corridor.

"Quick!" hissed Jess. "Hide!"

"Where?" said Flo.

Jess looked about her. "Here!" She dived in among the costumes on the clothes rail. Flo followed. Jess hoped they'd look just like clothes hanging up.

30

The dressing-room door banged open and a woman strode in, followed by the grumpy man who had come to their ballet class. "Julian Joompalot!" whispered Flo.

"And I bet that's Tanya Turnova," Jess whispered back.

"Just remember, darling," Tanya

was saying, "you must wait for the last scene. When you lift Margot high in the air, make it look as if you trip and then drop her. She's such a silly fool she's bound to twist her ankle. And tomorrow night *I'll* be the princess and *I'll* be the star!"

Tanya smiled a triumphant smile that made Jess shiver. Julian, who was still looking grumpy, nodded and left the room.

"Now, where's my tutu for Act Two?" muttered Tanya, turning to the clothes rail. Jess held her breath. She didn't dare move. Tanya looked along the rail. Suddenly she tweaked Jess's sleeve. "What are these disgusting things? They must be costumes from some dreadful play, put here by mistake." She scowled. "That wardrobe mistress needs a good talking-to!" And, to Jess's relief, Tanya turned on her heel and marched out of the room.

"A near miss," said Jess,

scrambling out from among the costumes.

"Especially since – look!" said Flo. "We're almost visible again."

It was true: the spell was wearing off. Jess could see Flo's nose and part of her hair, and when she

looked at herself in the mirror, she
had one eye and one ear, though
they were still a bit see-through.

"Come on!" said Flo, hurrying to
the door. "We must go and tell the
Miss Twirls what Tanya said."

When Jess and Flo arrived back at
Margot's dressing room, they found

Miss Ethel and Miss Angelica
already there. By now Miss
Angelica's disappearing spell had
worn off completely.

"We know Tanya's plan!"
gasped Jess, still out of breath from
running down the stairs.

"Tell us, quickly!" Miss Ethel
urged.

Jess repeated what they had heard Tanya say to Julian.

"He's going to *drop* Margot?" gasped Miss Angelica.

Margot's chin was trembling. "But I can't refuse to dance in the last scene," she said. "So how can I stop him?"

There was a silence. Jess and Flo looked at each other and then at the Miss Twirls. At last Miss Ethel said, "You don't have to do anything, Margot. Angelica – you take Jessica and Florence to their seats. They've done enough detective work for one evening and now they should enjoy the ballet. Leave Julian Joompalot to me."

"What will you do?" asked

Margot. But Miss Ethel had
already left the room.

Jess and Flo settled into their seats
with the rest of the audience. Jess
could see Primrose Pettifer and her

parents up in their box. She heard
Primrose say, "Where have *they*
been? Trust them to be late."

Miss Ethel's empty seat was next
to Jess.

"She'll miss the beginning if she's

not careful," said Flo. "See – the
conductor's coming out."

But then, just as the lights went
down and the orchestra was about
to start playing the *Sleeping Beauty*
music, Miss Ethel squeezed along

the row to her seat. Up above, Primrose tutted loudly.

Miss Ethel gave Jess and Flo the thumbs-up. There was no time to ask questions: the music began and, a few moments later, the curtain rose.

The ballet was wonderful. The costumes sparkled under the stage lights. The dancers leapt and spun and did lots of tricky steps. Margot Fountain danced beautifully as the princess, though sometimes she looked a little nervous. And when the wicked fairy came on stage, Flo clutched Jess's hand in fright. Jess heard Miss Ethel sigh. "Lovely story," she said, "but it gives magic *such* a bad name."

At last it was time for the final scene. Margot had a long dance to do with Julian Joompalot, who was playing the prince. Flo whispered, "This must be it!"

Jess looked at Miss Ethel. She

was watching the stage with fierce
concentration.

Holding her breath, Jess turned
back to watch the dancers too. At
one moment, when Julian was
holding Margot high above his

head, it looked as if he tripped. Jess gasped. But Julian didn't drop Margot. In fact, from that time on, he didn't put her down. He kept lowering her to the floor but, each time, she bobbed back up into the air again. His arms jerked, as if he was trying to tug his hands off her waist, but they wouldn't come free. Jess saw Julian look puzzled and then desperate. He had gone very red and was puffing and sweating. It looked very funny.

Margot seemed puzzled at first too, but then she remembered she was supposed to be smiling for the audience, and she made up some new steps while she waited for Julian to put her down.

He didn't. For the whole of the
rest of the ballet Margot remained
stuck to Julian's hands, and stuck in
the air. Tanya Turnova, who was

one of the princess's servants, was
looking furious.

It was a good job that it was the
last scene. Only when the music
stopped and the curtain came down
did Margot come down to earth
too. When the curtain rose again

for the dancers to take their bows,
Jess saw Julian stagger off stage.
Then she noticed that the gloves
he'd been wearing were still stuck to
Margot's costume. Jess giggled.
"You put a spell on his gloves!" she
said to Miss Ethel.

"Just a little one." Miss Ethel smiled proudly.

The rest of the audience were clapping and cheering. The director of the National Ballet came on to the stage and told the audience that Margot Fountain was the best Sleeping Beauty he had ever seen. Then Margot beckoned to the Miss Twirls to come up on stage and take a bow too.

"Come along, dears," said Miss Ethel as she took Jess's hand and Miss Angelica took Flo's.

"U-us? Go up there?" stammered Flo.

"Margot is thanking us for helping her tonight," said Miss Angelica. "You girls discovered

Tanya's plan. You must take a bow too."

So Jess and Flo and the Miss Twirls climbed the steps to the stage and took a bow with Margot

Fountain. She presented them each with a flower from her bouquet.

"I'm so happy, I think I'll explode!" said Flo.

Jess's grin was wide enough to make her face ache. This was her first trip to see a ballet and now she was on stage, taking a bow! She could see Primrose, up in her box, looking green with envy.

Some time later, Jess and Flo squashed themselves into the Miss Twirls' little car, and they set off for home.

"All's well that ends well," said Miss Angelica happily.

"So nice to see an old pupil again," beamed Miss Ethel.

"Will you have to go to the theatre every night," asked Jess, "in case Julian Joompalot tries to cause trouble again?"

Miss Ethel shook her head. "He won't get the chance, dear," she

said. "The director thought he'd
forgotten all his steps in the last
scene. He's been sacked. Margot
will have a different partner
tomorrow."

Just then the car stopped at some

traffic lights. "Look, Jess!" said Flo,
and pointed.

Jess looked out of the window.
Another car had stopped beside
them. It was large and black and
expensive looking. In the back sat a

girl in a smart party dress. It was
Primrose.

"What a car," sighed Flo.

Jess smiled. "We ought to thank
Primrose, I suppose."

"What on earth for?" said Flo.

"For not letting us ride with her

to the theatre, of course," said Jess.
She laughed. "If she'd said yes, we
wouldn't have had half such a
magical night, would we?"